The Emperor's Army

The EMPEROR'S ARMY

Virginia Walton Pilegard

Illustrated by
Adrian Tans

PELICAN PUBLISHING COMPANY
GRETNA 2010

Library of Congress Cataloging-in-Publication Data

Pilegard, Virginia Walton.
 The emperor's army / by Virginia Walton Pilegard ; illustrated by Adrian Tans.
    p. cm.
  Summary: In the second century, B.C., a scholar and his son are forced to flee the palace of China's first emperor, and while living in exile the boy discovers that a great terra-cotta army is being built.
  ISBN 978-1-58980-690-0 (alk. paper)
 1. China—History—Qin dynasty, 221-207 B.C.—Juvenile fiction. [1. China—History—Qin dynasty, 221-207 B.C.—Fiction. 2. Scholars—Fiction. 3. Statues—Fiction. 4. Qin shi huang, Emperor of China, 259-210 B.C.—Fiction. 5. Kings, queens, rulers, etc.—Fiction.] I. Tans, Adrian, ill. II. Title.
  PZ7.P6283Emp 2010
  [E]—dc22
                              2009030291

Printed in Singapore
Published by Pelican Publishing Company, Inc.
1000 Burmaster Street, Gretna, Louisiana 70053

Many years ago, a wise scholar and his son lived in the palace of China's first emperor, Qin Shi Huang. The scholar spent his days bringing the emperor armloads of reports written on strips of bamboo and bound with silk thread. At night, he would tell his son stories of their ruler who had come to power at just thirteen years of age.

"The First Emperor is a military genius," the scholar would say. "His armies have conquered six states. To unify his empire, he forces everyone to use the same style of writing and the same weights and measures. Even cart axles must all be the same width to match his new roads." Then the scholar would frown. "But I fear our emperor is becoming more influenced by his prime minister—an evil man who is jealous of scholars."

One evening the scholar rushed home. "We are in terrible danger," he cried. "Scholars are being buried alive!" He tossed their belongings into a bag. "All books except those on farming and medicine are to be burned!" With trembling hands, he packed all the books they could carry.

They fled to a cave on the side of Mount Li.

How their lives changed! Each day they sat together at the mouth of the cave enjoying the sunshine that filtered in through the flowering branches. The scholar would read, and the boy would do lessons from *Nine Chapters on the Mathematical Art*.

Once a week, the boy slipped down to the market to buy their meager supplies.

"What rumors do you hear in the marketplace?" the scholar asked one morning.

"More artists are accused of disagreeing with the emperor and arrested each day," the boy answered, "and a giant hole for the excavation of clay grows deep enough to make a lake."

"What could our emperor be building?" the scholar mused.

"I have heard of the many roads and canals the emperor builds to connect the lands he conquers—even a great wall to protect him from his enemies in the north," the boy offered.

"It does not take skilled artists to build roads or canals, or even great walls." The scholar shook his head. "What strange project does he undertake now?"

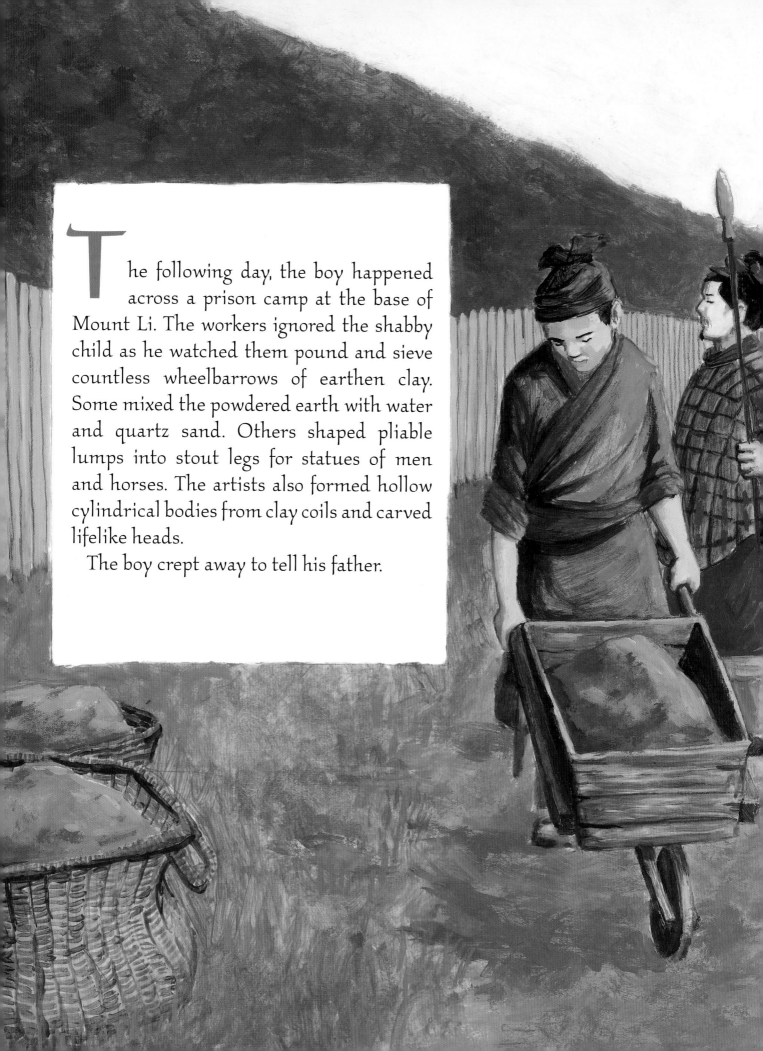

The following day, the boy happened across a prison camp at the base of Mount Li. The workers ignored the shabby child as he watched them pound and sieve countless wheelbarrows of earthen clay. Some mixed the powdered earth with water and quartz sand. Others shaped pliable lumps into stout legs for statues of men and horses. The artists also formed hollow cylindrical bodies from clay coils and carved lifelike heads.

The boy crept away to tell his father.

"Can you estimate the total number of statues?" the scholar challenged his son.

The boy smiled. "I estimate each wheelbarrow carries four cubic feet of earth, more than enough for one statue. I have only to determine how many cubic feet of earthen clay have been mined from the big hole where they work to estimate the number of statues."

On his next trip to the market, the boy hurried to the clay mine to make his calculations. He stepped off the length and the width of the hole. He counted his sliding steps down the hole's steep side. However, when the boy arrived at the village, thoughts of mathematics were swept from his mind.

"The emperor is dead!" a man shouted.

The boy ran to the cave to tell his father.

"And now the emperor's oldest son will rule," the scholar said.

"That is the oddest part." The boy scratched his chin. "His oldest son has died. It is whispered the prime minister tricked the first son into killing himself because he could better control the weaker second son."

"That is unfortunate," the scholar replied. "The second son has all of his father's ruthlessness, but none of his genius."

S oon, food became scarce in the market. People complained too many peasants had been taken from their farms at the whim of the emperor, and not enough were left to grow crops. Murmured complaints turned to open talk of rebellion.

One morning, the scholar and his son spied a column of dust far below them. They slipped into the cave to stash their precious books under a covering of reeds.

The mountain trembled with the approach of marching feet.

"Come out, Wise One!" a rough voice called.

After a moment's silence, men rushed into the cave and dragged the scholar and his son into the bright daylight.

The scholar shook himself free and peered at the intruders, a ragged band of men. "Who are you, and why do you bother a poor hermit and his child?"

"We are the peasants who will overthrow an empire. We have the righteous anger. We need money for weapons. You must help us." The man who seemed to lead the band spoke again in his gruff voice. "Enough treasure to finance our entire rebellion must be buried with the First Emperor."

"But the site of his grave is a terrible secret," the scholar said. "I fear many men have died to keep it so."

The boy tugged at his father's sleeve. "Perhaps the emperor was buried near the prison camp I visited. Perhaps the statues were for his grave."

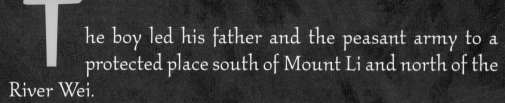

The boy led his father and the peasant army to a protected place south of Mount Li and north of the River Wei.

"This would be an auspicious place to bury an important man," the scholar announced.

Everyone began to dig furiously.

Soon after the digging began, the group shouted with excitement upon the discovery of an underground chamber. But their joy quickly turned to shrieks of terror! Tumbling down a long ramp, the intruders found themselves looking down on a mighty army. The first row of archers knelt with their bows. Rows of infantry and cavalry soldiers stood at the ready behind them.

The boy stared in wonder. "Wait," he cried as the peasant soldiers scrambled to flee. "These soldiers are made of clay! I saw them being created."

Muttering with anger, the peasants turned to face the emperor's terracotta army.

"Look at their weapons," the leader gasped. "Real bows and spears and swords!"

The scholar tossed a fine silk scarf into the air. It fell onto one of the clay soldier's swords and was sliced cleanly in half. "These are made of the finest metal alloy. Their blades will stay sharp for two thousand years or more," he said in awe. "The emperor must have had this army built to guard him in the afterlife."

He turned to his son. "Though they were enslaved, the artists took great pride in their work."

The boy and his father studied the statues; each skillfully carved face was unique. And, oh, the colors of their garb— bright reds and yellows, greens and blues, blacks and browns. At the corridor's end, a proud-faced charioteer drove a team of lifelike horses from the seat of a chariot decorated with gold and silver ornaments.

However, these soldiers were no match for an army of flesh and blood. The boy watched the intruders grab the statues' weapons and set fire to the earthen pit's wooden supports.

"There must be other pits with more statues," the boy exclaimed. "I measured the hole where this clay was mined. I multiplied its length times its width times its depth. I estimate it must have contained well over 34,000 cubic feet. When I divide 34,000 cubic feet of clay by the four-cubic-foot wheelbarrow load needed for each statue, the quotient is 8,500. I am guessing they made at least 8,000 statues. That would leave some clay for bricks and other pottery objects."

When more buried statues were discovered as the boy predicted, the scholar's eyes smiled with pride.

"You are a clever boy," the gruff-voiced leader said. He rewarded the scholar and his son with a fine house in the village where they lived the rest of their lives openly studying their beloved books.

On March 29, 1974, Chinese farmers drilling for water discovered the terra-cotta army on which our story is based. These statues of the elite fighting force led by the First Emperor are found in underground corridors divided by earth-rammed partition walls and paved with bricks. Placed in defensive position with regard to his actual tomb, the army was built to protect Emperor Qin Shi Huang in the afterlife. According to the ancient Chinese book *Records of the Grand Historian*, rebel peasant armies burned the emperor's palace in 206 B.C. The terra-cotta army is believed to have been vandalized at that time.

Painstakingly restored, the terra-cotta warriors and their horses and chariots are considered by many to be the eighth wonder of the world. In 2009, Chinese archaeologists began a five-year excavation of the terra-cotta army site, hoping to unearth more clay figures.

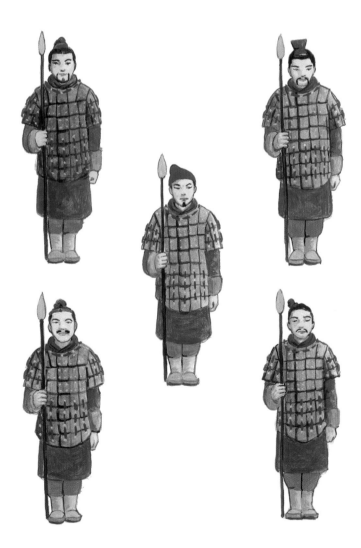

To create your own "clay" statue, combine 2 cups white flour with 1 cup table salt. Add ¾ cup warm water and 2 teaspoons cooking oil.

Can you estimate how many ½-cup statues you will be able to create?

Shape the dough into a ball and knead for ten minutes. Create your statues on a foil-covered cookie sheet, "gluing" pieces together with dabs of water. Carve features into your soldiers with a toothpick.

Bake overnight or until completely hardened in a 225-degree oven. Cool with the oven door closed.

Was your estimation correct?